GRAPHIC SHAKESPEARE
JULIUS CAESAR CANCELLED

CONTENTS

Published by
Evans Brothers Limited
2A Portman Mansions
Chiltern Street
London W1M 1LE

© in the modern text Hilary Burningham 1997
© in the illustrations Evans Brothers Ltd 1997
Designed by Design Systems Ltd.

British Library Cataloguing in Publication Data
Burningham, Hilary
 Julius Caesar
 Teacher's book. – (The graphic Shakespeare series)
 1. Shakespeare, William, 1564-1616. Julius Caesar
 2. Shakespeare, William, 1564-1616. – Study and teaching
 (Secondary)
 I. Title II. May, Dan
 822.3'3

 ISBN 0 237 51792 2

Printed in Hong Kong by Wing King Tong Co. Ltd.

INTRODUCTION TO
THE GRAPHIC JULIUS CAESAR ACTIVITY BOOK

The graphic text

The purpose of the graphic text is to involve pupils in the excitement and the drama of *Julius Caesar*. The story is told in straightforward, accessible language that nevertheless brings out the conflicts of personality and the dramatic twists of the plot that are an essential part of Shakespeare.

Each page features a Key Speech, Shakespeare's words, of particular relevance to that portion of the graphic text. Pupils have an opportunity to become familiar with Shakespeare's language in a simple, uncluttered presentation.

There can be no substitute for the excitement of a Shakespeare play performed live on stage. *The Graphic Shakespeare* attempts to make his work more accessible to young readers representing varied cultural backgrounds and levels of ability so that they will be encouraged to explore further, developing their appreciation and new skills in the process.

The student activities

The majority of the photocopiable activities provided in this book are sufficiently straightforward to enable any pupil to work independently and produce a respectable piece of work. In some activities, sentences are provided for completion; in others, questions are closely matched to the text to facilitate the pupil response. The advantage of this very basic approach is that it helps pupils to become accustomed to correct usage. At a certain stage in language development, particularly for those using English as a second or other language, struggling with open questions may lead to the reinforcement of past mistakes, or to frustration when trying to produce original writing without having acquired the skills to do so. As students progress, they will find additional suggestions and opportunities for more demanding work.

It is not expected that every pupil will complete every activity in the book. Rather, it is the intention to provide manageable tasks at each stage of the play so that the teacher has available suitable materials for the pupils who need them.

It is suggested that pupils use a separate notebook for the written activities. This notebook will provide a good framework for revision.

Attainment levels

In keeping with the aims of the National Curriculum, and to promote effective monitoring and record-keeping in line with the Special Needs Code of Practice, appropriate attainment levels are suggested for each activity.

It should be noted that in general the attainment levels given for Reading (Attainment Target 2) are higher than those for Writing (AT 3). This is because Shakespeare's text, even with the aids and prompts that are given, demands a good level of reading comprehension. Keeping in mind that AT 2 emphasises responses to a range of texts, the work on Shakespeare needs to be seen as part of the balanced selection of literature that the pupil will study in the course of the year. Understanding Shakespeare's language will contribute to the pupil's attaining up to Level 5.

Higher levels in AT 3 can be achieved by providing opportunities for original writing as and when pupils have the necessary skills. Suggestions and ideas for more demanding work are included with many of the activities.

Speaking and listening

Given the emphasis in the National Curriculum on Speaking and Listening, Attainment Target 1, it is desirable that pupils be encouraged to work 'with a partner' or 'in small groups' whenever possible in order to promote verbal and aural skills, particularly in the art of reading/speaking Shakespeare's language.

The idea of *mime* is introduced as the first activity to promote the use of actions and gestures as part of the acting process. It is also effective as a loosening-up technique to encourage pupils to get involved in the drama.

Pupils will often need to be reminded of the importance of how they move on stage and it may be helpful to do other scenes in this way. Mime is suggested as a way of working through the assassination scene, while Mark Antony's funeral speech, for example, could also be acted silently through gesture and movement, with the crowd similarly miming their response.

In addition to the Key Speeches featured in the Graphic text, Key Scenes or groups of speeches feature in the activities with the original text beside a modern, paraphrased version - giving pupils the option of experimenting with the dialogue in contemporary English before moving to Shakespeare's English. (More able pupils will enjoy doing their own paraphrasing. It is an old-fashioned but still extremely useful technique.)

The device of *'The Karate Kid'* (page 45) gives 'street cred' to peer group teaching! *Karate Kids* and their *senseis* can work together to paraphrase additional speeches, compare and revise pieces of original writing, or prepare scenes for class presentation. Senseis should be warmly praised when their 'pupils' do well.

The *'Who Am I?'* game (page 38) is an excellent revision technique, once the pupils have an overview of the play. It also promotes discussion in line with Attainment Target 1. To play, pupils will need copies of the rules (page 38), the *'Character Clues'* (pages 39-41) and the *Picture Gallery* (page 42). The *'Character Clues'* can be used in several ways. First, in preparation for the *'Who Am I?'* game, portraits from the *Picture Gallery* need to be matched to the cards. In a turnaround, the portraits alone can appear on the cards, and pupils are invited to write their own sets of 'clues'.

Uses of the key speeches
Key Speeches can be used in several ways. First, to gain an understanding of and a feeling for Shakespeare's language. Second, to gain practice in speaking Shakespeare's lines. Speeches from the worksheets can be photocopied, and the appropriate lines copied or pasted onto card. Pupils can then practise reading them aloud with appropriate expression, in small, manageable sections. Some lines can often be committed to memory in this way.

Portraits from the *Picture Gallery* (page 42) can be matched with short excerpts from the Key Speeches under the heading of *'Did I Say That?'* or *'Who Said That?'*

About the newspaper
Under the National Curriculum, pupils will look at different styles of newspapers. The device of the tabloid is used here (pages 26-30) because it provides an immediate and vivid way of presenting Caesar's murder and the funeral speeches. The four pages 27-30, photocopied on A3 or A4 paper taped together, make a reasonable facsimile of a tabloid. The pupil can use the sentences provided or produce a piece of original work. The activity is intended to raise awareness of the impact of these shattering events on the wider population. The pupil is encouraged to identify with the person on the street or, as in the diaries, with the ordinary foot soldier.

The teacher may wish to discuss why a headline writer would choose to write, 'CAESAR SLAIN!' rather than, 'CAESAR MURDERED!' Headlines appear again in the activity *'You Are the Editor'* on pages 43 and 44.

The pupil record sheet
The pupil record sheet *Record of my Work*, page 47, provides an all-important opportunity for self-assessment. The pupil enters the number and title of the sheet, together with an indication of how well it was completed. The pupil then also assesses the degree of ease or difficulty of each activity. If he or she is ticking too many 'easy' boxes, it is time to move to more challenging work. There is a final column where the teacher may wish to enter comments when appropriate. Pupils are also encouraged, on completion of the unit on *Julius Caesar*, to assess and comment on the outcomes on the sheet *What Things Have Improved?* on page 48.

THE TRIBUNES

This activity is aimed to help you to become an actor!
Form yourselves into acting groups of four or five and read together pages 6 and 8
of your *Graphic Julius Caesar*.

You are going to mime this scene. That means that you are going to act it out without words.

First, decide who will take the parts of the important men (tribunes), Flavius and Marullus, and who will be the workmen (two or three of you).

Working without words, but with large gestures (actions), Flavius and Marullus and the workmen mime the action in the scene.

Clear a space in the classroom to be your 'stage'. Decide where the front of your stage is to be, facing the audience.

For example, your mime could go like this: (REMEMBER! You must not speak or make any sounds.)

The workmen enter, laughing and having a good time.

Flavius and Marullus come in from the opposite side and point angrily at the workmen, especially at their clothes.

The workmen are puzzled, scratch their heads, and look down at their clothes.

What are the tribunes angry about? The workmen look excited and pretend to cheer for Caesar.

Marullus becomes more angry and mimes cheering for Pompey. He points angrily off to the side for the workmen to go on their way.

Flavius too points the way off the stage. The workmen go, still looking puzzled.

Flavius and Marullus mime pulling the decorations off Caesar's statues, shake hands and go off in different directions.

When you have practised a few times, demonstrate your miming work to the rest of the class.

AT 2: Level 2-4

THE TRIBUNES AND THE TRADESMEN

Here are some speeches from the first scene of Act One. The words in italics are in modern speech, as we would speak today. Working in your groups, read them aloud with expression and feeling, first in modern English (*in italics*), then in Shakespeare's English. Try to use gestures, as you did in your mime.

Key Speeches

FLAVIUS:	Hence! Home, you idle creatures, get you home! Is this a holiday? What, know you not, Being mechanical, you ought not walk Upon a labouring day without the sign Of your profession? Speak, what trade art thou?	*Go away, you lazy people, go home! Is this some sort of holiday? Don't you know that you are workmen, and on a workday you should wear your work clothes? Tell me, what is your work?*
CARPENTER:	Why, sir, a carpenter.	*I am a carpenter, sir.*
MARULLUS:	Where is thy leather apron and thy rule? What dost thou with thy best apparel on? You, sir, what trade are you?	*Where is your leather apron and your ruler? What are you doing with your best clothes on? [To the next man] What is your trade?*
COBBLER:	Truly, sir, in respect of a fine workman, I am but, as you would say, a cobbler.	*Compared to a very skilled workman, I am only a cobbler.*
MARULLUS:	But what trade art thou? Answer me directly.	*[Thinks he is joking, and gets impatient] But what is your trade? Answer me clearly.*
COBBLER:	A trade, sir, that, I hope, I may use with a safe conscience, which is indeed, sir, a mender of bad soles.	*A good trade - I mend bad soles.*[1]
MARULLUS:	And do you now put on your best attire? And do you now cull out a holiday? And do you now strew flowers in his way That comes in triumph over Pompey's blood? Be gone!	*And are you wearing your best clothes and giving yourselves a holiday and throwing flowers down in front of the man who is celebrating killing Pompey? Go away!*
FLAVIUS:	...let no images Be hung with Caesar's trophies... These growing feathers plucked from Caesar's wing Will make him fly an ordinary pitch...	*The statues must not be decorated in honour of Caesar. If we can stop these honours for Caesar, it will stop him becoming so important.*

[1]This is called a pun, which means playing with words that sound the same but have different meanings. Soles can be the soles of shoes, or he could mean human souls. It would be a good trade to mend bad human souls!

AT 2: Level 2-5

FLAVIUS AND MARULLUS

You will need your notebook. Remember to write the date and the title at the beginning of each new piece of work. Decide which word(s) best complete each sentence, and write the sentence in your notebook. You will find the answers on pages 6 and 8 of your *Graphic Julius Caesar*.

1. Flavius and Marullus were (*soldiers farmers tribunes*).

2. The Feast of Lupercal was a (*sports religious school*) day.

3. The workmen were dressed in their (*best working old*) clothes.

4. The workmen were celebrating (*Pompey's Marullus' Caesar's*) victory.

5. Caesar had beaten Pompey, who was also a famous (*Englishman Roman Frenchman*).

6. Flavius and Marullus were (*happy sad angry*) that the people liked Caesar so much.

7. They told the workmen to go (*to town to the country to their homes*).

8. Flavius and Marullus decided to pull the (*arms decorations heads*) off the statues of Caesar.

When you have done these, work with a partner and try making up some more sentences in the same way. The new sentences can be about anything you like, but be sure to include a set of words from which to choose. Ask another group to try to do your sentences.

AT 2: Level 3
AT 3: Level 2-3

THE SOOTHSAYER'S WARNING

Work in groups of five. Decide who is to take the parts of Casca, Caesar, the Soothsayer, Brutus and Cassius. Read the speeches in modern English, then in Shakespeare's English. Think about how the Soothsayer would call out to get Caesar's attention. Caesar says his voice is shrill, which means high-pitched. When you have practised the speeches, act out the scene for the rest of the class. Ask the class to be the crowd, cheering for Caesar. Remember that the Soothsayer should start out as a member of the crowd.

Key Speeches

SOOTHSAYER:	Caesar!	
CAESAR:	Ha! Who calls?	
CASCA:	Bid every noise be still; peace yet again.	*Silence, everybody; quiet, please.*
CAESAR:	Who is it in the press that calls on me? I hear a tongue, shriller than all the music, Cry 'Caesar'. Speak; Caesar is turned to hear.	*Who in the crowd is calling to me? I hear a voice that is higher than all the music shouting, 'Caesar'. Speak, I'm listening.*
SOOTHSAYER:	Beware the ides of March.	*Be careful on the fifteenth of March.*
CAESAR:	What man is that?	*Who is this person?*
BRUTUS:	A soothsayer[1] bids you beware the ides of March.	*A prophet[1] is asking you to be careful on the fifteenth of March.*
CAESAR:	Set him before me; let me see his face.	*Bring him in front of me; let me see his face.*
CASSIUS:	Fellow, come from the throng; look upon Caesar.	*You, step out of the crowd; come in front of Caesar.*
CAESAR:	What say'st thou to me now? Speak once again.	*What are you saying to me? Say it again.*
SOOTHSAYER:	Beware the ides of March.	*Be careful on the fifteenth of March.*
CAESAR:	He is a dreamer, let us leave him. Pass.	*He is imagining things, let's go. Move on.*

Write the following sentences in your notebook and decide whether they are True or False.

1. The soothsayer had a low, quiet voice. *(True, False)*
2. Caesar wouldn't listen to the soothsayer. *(True, False)*
3. Caesar said the soothsayer was crazy. *(True, False)*
4. Brutus heard the soothsayer's warning. *(True, False)*
5. Cassius and Casca heard the soothsayer's warning. *(True, False)*

[1] soothsayer/prophet – person who can see into the future.

AT 2: Level 2-5
AT 3: Level 2-3

BRUTUS AND CASSIUS

> Read page 12 of the *Graphic Julius Caesar*. Complete the following sentences
> in your notebook. Have you written the date and the title?

1. Brutus admitted that he _____ _____.

2. In Rome, the power of the government was shared _____ _____ _____.

3. Brutus did not want one man _____ _____ _____ _____ _____.

4. Cassius and Brutus could hear _____ _____ _____.

5. Cassius told Brutus _____ _____.

6. Cassius tried to make Caesar seem _____ and _____.

7. Brutus agreed to think about _____ _____ _____ _____ _____.

8. Cassius was _____ _____.

> Read these speeches with a partner. Take turns being Brutus and Cassius.

Key Speeches

BRUTUS: What means this shouting?   *What is that shouting all about? I am*
                  I do fear the people   *afraid the people are asking Caesar to be*
                  Choose Caesar for their king.   *their king.*

CASSIUS: Ay, do you fear it?   *Oh, you are afraid of that? Then that gives*
                  Then must I think you would not have it so.   *me the idea that you don't want Caesar to*
                                                             be king.

BRUTUS: I would not, Cassius, yet I love him well.   *I don't want it, Cassius, even though I love*
                  But wherefore do you hold me here so long?   *Caesar.*
                  What is it that you would impart to me?   *But why are you keeping me here?*
                                                          What do you want to tell me?

AT 2: Level 2-3
AT 3: Level 2-3

CASSIUS: A DANGEROUS MAN?

> Written below is what Caesar and Mark Antony are saying in the picture.
> The words in italics are how we might speak today. Read the speeches with a partner in modern language, then in Shakespeare's language.
>
> Next, paste or draw the picture in your notebook. In each of the speech bubbles write a few words to give the idea of what is being said.

CAESAR: Let me have men about me that are fat,
Sleek-headed men, and such as sleep a-nights.
Yond Cassius has a lean and hungry look;
He thinks too much: such men are dangerous.

I like to have people around me that are fat and well-groomed, who sleep well at night. Cassius over there looks thin and hungry; he thinks too much: people like that are dangerous.

ANTONY: Fear him not, Caesar, he's not dangerous;
He is a noble Roman, and well-given.

Don't be afraid of him, Caesar, he isn't dangerous. He's a good Roman, with a good character.

CAESAR: Would he were fatter! But I fear him not.
Yet if my name were liable to fear,
I do not know the man I should avoid
So soon as that spare Cassius. He reads much,
He is a great observer, and he looks
Quite through the deeds of men.

I still wish he were fatter! But I am not afraid of him. Even so, if I were the kind of person to be afraid, I would avoid that skinny Cassius more that anyone. He reads a lot, he watches everything closely and he sees the hidden reasons for our actions.

Caesar's speech bubble might say: Cassius is too thin and thinks too much. He's dangerous.

Mark Antony - Don't worry. He's a good Roman.

AT 2: Level 2-5

CASCA'S STORY

> For this, you need to work in groups of three. Read page 16 of the *Graphic Julius Caesar*
> aloud in your groups. Decide who will be Brutus, Cassius and Casca.

Casca is to describe the scene in the marketplace to Brutus and Cassius. Brutus and Cassius will ask him questions to get the whole story.

Remember that Casca was disgusted that the people were offering Caesar a crown. Try to make your audience understand his feelings.

Example:

CASSIUS or BRUTUS
might say: *Casca, you were in the market place. We heard shouting and cheering. What*
                            was happening?

CASCA: *Oh, such a lot of daft things going on. You wouldn't believe it. Everyone was*
                            shouting and praising Caesar. Mark Antony offered him a crown! Three times
                            he offered it. Three times Caesar pushed it away. But it seemed to me he
                            really wanted to take it.

CASSIUS or BRUTUS: *Then what happened?*

CASCA: *When he refused it the third time, all the people shouted and clapped their*
                            hands and threw their dirty hats in the air and Caesar almost choked on their
                            bad-smelling breath. He fainted and fell down. As for me, I didn't dare open
                            my mouth. I didn't want to breathe in that bad air.

Casca's Speech

Here is what Casca actually says in the play. Now try reading it with expression. Remember, Casca thought this was really a lot of nonsense.

CASCA: I can as well be hanged as tell the manner of it: it was mere foolery: I did not mark it. I saw Mark Antony offer him a crown--yet 'twas not a crown neither, 'twas one of these coronets -- and, as I told you, he put it by at once; but for all that, to my thinking, he would fain have had it. Then he offered it to him again; then he put it by again; but to my thinking, he was very loath to lay his fingers off it. And then he offered it the third time.

He put it the third time by; and still as he refused it, the rabblement hooted, and clapped their chopt hands, and threw up their sweaty nightcaps, and uttered such a deal of stinking breath because Caesar refused the crown, that it had, almost, choked Caesar; for he swounded and fell down at it. And for mine own part, I durst not laugh, for fear of opening my lips and receiving the bad air.

AT 1: Level 2-4
AT 2: Level 4-5

CAN YOU FILL IN CASSIUS'S THOUGHTS?

Read page 19 of the *Graphic Julius Caesar*. Choose the words that best complete Cassius's thoughts, below, and write them in the spaces. When you have finished and checked your work, paste the page in your notebook.

Brutus is a very _____ man, and a loyal _____ to Caesar. Yet he loves _____ more than anything else.

I think I'll write some _____ to him, pretending that they have been written by _____ people of Rome. The letters will say that _____ is a famous man and Romans look to him for _____ . He must stop Caesar getting so _____ .

I'm sure that if Brutus gets _____ like that, we can convince him to help us to stop _____ .

good   friend   Rome

letters   ordinary   Brutus   leadership

powerful   letters   Caesar

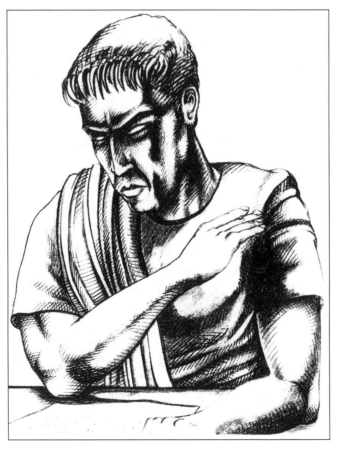

CASSIUS

AT 2: Level 2-4

CASSIUS'S PLAN

With a partner, read page 19 of the *Graphic Julius Caesar* aloud. Talk about Cassius's plan.

CASSIUS:

...I will this night
In several hands, in at his windows throw,
As if they came from several citizens,
Writings, all tending to the great opinion
That Rome holds of his name...
And after this, let Caesar seat him sure;
For we will shake him, or worse days endure.

Tonight I will throw in Brutus's window several letters in different handwritings as though they came from different citizens, all about how his fellow Romans admire Brutus. And then, Caesar had better be careful, for we will get rid of him, or there will be bad days ahead for all of us.

Now, write a letter to Brutus like the ones Cassius was planning to write. Make your letter look as real as possible.

To help you, here are some sentences that Cassius might have used. Can you put them in a sensible order?

Caesar is getting too powerful.

You are a brave man.

Dear Brutus

What are you going to do about it?

You are a great leader. The people will follow you.

I am an ordinary citizen.

It is not right that one man should have all the power.

I am very worried about what is happening in Rome.

I think Caesar's power should be taken away.

Romans have never wanted to have a king!

Yours sincerely, A Worried Citizen

AT 3: Level 2-3

THE CONSPIRATORS NEEDED BRUTUS

With a partner read pages 22 and 23 in the *Graphic Julius Caesar* together.
Talk about how best to answer the questions below.
Write the answers in good sentences in your books.

1.   What does the word *conspirator* mean?

2.   Who were the three main conspirators?

3.   Why did they need Brutus to join the plot?

   a) _____

   b) _____

   c) _____

4.   Cassius gave Cinna three fake letters. Where was Cinna to put them?
      (Look at Cassius' instructions in the Key Speech below.)

   a) _____

   b) _____

   c) _____

CASSIUS:

Good Cinna, take this paper,
And look you lay it in the praetor's chair,
Where Brutus may but find it; and throw this
In at his window; set this up with wax
Upon old Brutus' statue. All this done,
Repair to Pompey's porch, where you shall
find us.

*Good Cinna, take this letter
and be sure to put it in the Chief
Magistrate's chair, where only Brutus will
find it; and throw this one in at his
window; and stick this one with sealing
wax to the statue of old Brutus[1]. When you
have done all those things, go to Pompey's
porch, where we shall all meet.*

[1]old Brutus – a member of Brutus' family who lived many years before. He was one of the founders of Rome.

AT 2: Level 2-4
AT 3: Level 2-3

PROBLEMS FOR BRUTUS

Cassius had told Brutus many bad things about Caesar. Brutus had to decide what to do.

Make two columns with these headings:

REASONS TO STOP CAESAR	REASONS NOT TO GET INVOLVED

Put the reasons under the heading where they belong:

Caesar is my friend. He trusts me.

Caesar is too ambitious.

We Romans have never had a king. Caesar seems to want to be King.

I would be hurting my own friend.

Caesar is a good general. He has won many battles for Rome.

Caesar fought against Pompey, a fellow Roman.

Now I even have a letter asking me to stop Caesar.

Can you think of any other reasons to put under either heading?

Here is another one: Brutus was very proud of his family and his ancestors.

BRUTUS: My ancestors did from the streets of Rome
The Tarquin drive, when he was called a king.
'Speak, strike, redress.' Am I entreated
To speak and strike? O Rome, I make thee promise,
If the redress will follow, thou receivest
Thy full petition at the hand of Brutus!

Many years ago members of my family helped to get rid of invaders who wanted to rule over Rome. 'Speak out, do something, make things fair again.' [He is reading the letter] Am I begged to do these things? I promise Rome, if it will help to change this situation, I will do as I am asked.

So, another reason would be:

Fighting for Rome is a tradition in my family.

AT 2: Level 2-5

THE IDES OF MARCH

Write the following in your notebook. Notes like this help you to revise
(learn your work before an examination). You may need to look back at page 10 as well as
page 24 in the *Graphic Julius Caesar*.

---

1.   Lucius told Brutus that the next day was the _____ ____ _____.

2.   A soothsayer was a person who _____.

3.   The soothsayer's warning to Caesar was, '_____ _____ _____ ____ _____'.

4.   The ides of March meant the _____ day of March.

Brutus joined the conspirators (page 26)

Should they swear an oath?

5.   What is an **oath**?

6.   Who wanted the conspirators to swear an oath?

7.   Who did not want the conspirators to swear an oath?

Look at Brutus's Key Speech:

BRUTUS: What other bond
             Than secret Romans that have spoke the
             word,
             And will not palter? And what other oath
             Than honesty to honesty engaged?

*The only agreement that we need is that we
are Romans who can keep a secret and
having made up our minds will not change
our minds. What could be better than our
personal honour, man to man?*

8.   Did the conspirators swear an oath?

9.   Brutus said that they were all honest men. Do you agree?

AT 2: Level 2-5
AT 3: Level 2-3

DECISIONS FOR THE CONSPIRATORS

Should they kill only Caesar?

Should they kill Mark Antony as well?

> Draw two columns as below, and write the headings. Put Cassius's reasons and
> Brutus's reasons under the correct columns.

Brutus: Don't kill Mark Antony. Reasons:	Cassius: Kill Mark Antony. Reasons:

Mark Antony would be nothing without Caesar.

Mark Antony loved Caesar. He should die at the same time.

The conspirators would seem too 'bloody' if they killed both Caesar and Mark Antony.

Mark Antony could be very dangerous to the conspirators.

He could make a lot of trouble for them.

Key Speeches

CASSIUS
> I think it is not meet
> Mark Antony, so well beloved of Caesar,
> Should outlive Caesar; we shall find of him
> A shrewd contriver;

I think it is not right that Mark Antony whom Caesar cares for very much should live after Caesar; I think he could turn out to be very cunning.

BRUTUS:
> Our course will seem too bloody, Caius Cassius,
> To cut the head off and then hack the limbs,
> Like wrath in death and envy afterwards;
> For Antony is but a limb of Caesar.

We will seem to be too bloodthirsty, Caius Cassius, like cutting off the head of a man and then hacking his body to bits; we'll look as if we are killing Mark Antony just because we don't like him. Mark Antony will be useless without Caesar.

AT 2: Level 2-5

HOW WELL DO YOU KNOW THE CONSPIRATORS?

Brutus   Cassius   Cinna   Casca   Decius Brutus

> Cut out the pictures of five of the conspirators (above) and paste them into your
> notebook with four or five lines between each one. Write below the pictures the sentence(s)
> that fit each one. Some pictures will have more than one sentence.

1.   I was the leader of the conspirators until Brutus joined us.

2.   I told Brutus and Cassius what happened in the market place.

3.   I put three of Cassius' fake letters where Brutus would find them.

4.   I thought that Mark Antony should be killed as well as Caesar.

5.   I thought that Mark Antony was nothing without Caesar.

6.   I had to persuade Caesar to go to the Capitol so that we could murder him!

7.   I thought that the conspirators were all honest men. We did not need to swear an oath.

8.   I saw Mark Antony offer Caesar a crown in the market place.

9.   I received letters from the people of Rome. They wanted me to do something about Caesar. He was getting
       too powerful.

10.   I would have done anything to persuade Brutus to join our plan. We needed him!

Can you think of other sentences to write under the pictures?

AT 2: Level 3-4

CALPHURNIA'S DREAM

Look at pages 32 and 34 in the *Graphic Julius Caesar* to help you to answer the questions below.
Remember to answer in good sentences.

1.   What did Calphurnia call out in her sleep?

2.   Why was Calphurnia worried?

3.   What did Caesar agree to do?

Practise reading this speech aloud, in modern English and in Shakespeare's English.
Can you speak it from memory?

Key Speech

CAESAR:

Cowards die many times before their deaths;	*People who are afraid imagine their own*
The valiant never taste of death but once.	*death many times; brave people die only*
Of all the wonders that I yet have heard,	*when it actually happens to them. I have*
It seems to me most strange that men should	*heard many amazing things in my life, but*
fear,	*one of the strangest is that people should*
Seeing that death, a necessary end,	*be afraid of dying. We all have to die some*
Will come when it will come.	*time, and when it happens, it happens.*

Calphurnia's Dream: Caesar's statue was pouring blood and Romans were smiling and washing their hands in the blood.

An **interpretation** is an explanation of what the dream means. Here are two interpretations of Calphurnia's dream. Copy the interpretations and write Decius Brutus after one and Calphurnia after the other.

Interpretation 1.   *This is a terrible dream. It warns of evil, and dreadful things that will soon happen to Caesar.* _____.

Interpretation 2.   *This is a wonderful dream. It means that the people of Rome get their strength from Caesar. Important Romans will want to have any scraps from Caesar to remember him.* _____.

Note on **Irony**.

When the audience knows something that a character in the play doesn't know, we have irony. For example, Caesar greeted the conspirators:

> CAESAR: Good friends, go in and taste some wine with me,
> And we (like friends) will straightway go together.

*The audience knows that these men (except Mark Antony) are planning to murder Caesar. This moment in the play is full of **irony**. Can you find some other examples?*

AT 2: Level 2-5
AT 3: Level 2-4

TWO WARNINGS ON THE WAY TO THE CAPITOL

Cut out the picture below. Paste it in your book. In the speech balloons for each
character, carefully print in the three short speeches.

Artemidorus: Hail, Caesar! Read this schedule.

Caesar: The ides of March are come!

Soothsayer: Ay, Caesar, but not gone.

CAESAR'S MURDER • 1

Working on your own or with a partner, choose the correct words
from the brackets and write the sentences in your notebook. When you have finished,
make a diagram of the stage as shown below.

1. Caesar went to the (*Forum   Capitol   Arena*). He was surrounded by people asking him
    for (*food   money   favours*).

2. The person who first knelt in front of Caesar was called (*Metellus Cimber   Trebonius   Decius Brutus*).
    He wanted Caesar to let his (*aunt   sister   brother*) come back to Rome.

3. Two other people knelt in front of Caesar, begging him to change his mind.
    They were (*Trebonius   Cassius   Decius Brutus   Cinna   Brutus*).

4. Casca's signal to the conspirators was the words:

    "_____ _____ _____ _____ !"

5. When Caesar saw that Brutus stabbed him, he cried, ***Et tu, Brute?*** which means

    "_____ _____ , _____ ?"

Use the sentences above to work out a mime of Caesar's last moments.

Here is a diagram of the stage, showing where the key people were when Casca
gave the signal. Metellus Cimber, Cassius and Brutus were kneeling in front of Caesar.
The other conspirators would come forward and stab Caesar.

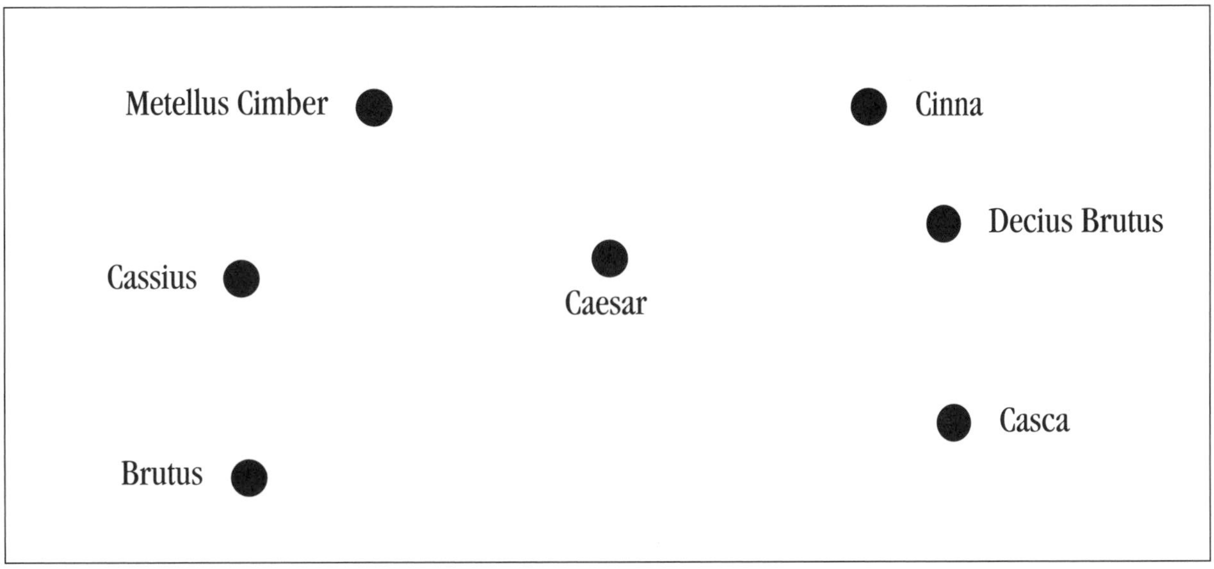

Metellus Cimber ●   ● Cinna

                                                ● Decius Brutus

Cassius ●

                        ●
                      Caesar

                                          ● Casca

Brutus ●

CAESAR'S MURDER • 2

Key Speech

> You need six people to take the parts of Caesar, Brutus, Cassius, Casca, Cinna and
> Metellus Cimber. Read the scene first in modern English (*italics*), then in Shakespeare's English.
> This scene should move very quickly.

CAESAR:
(to Metellus Cimber)

(Metellus Cimber is kneeling in front of Caesar)
Thy brother by decree is banished,
If thou doest bend and pray and fawn for him,
I spurn thee like a cur out of my way.
Know, Caesar doth not wrong, nor without cause
Will he be satisfied.

Your brother has been told to leave this country by law. If you kneel and grovel and try to get him special treatment, I shall kick you out of my way like a dog. I, Caesar, do not make mistakes and I shall not be satisfied until your brother has served his sentence

METELLUS:

Is there no voice more worthy than my own,
To sound more sweetly in great Caesar's ear
For the repealing of my banished brother?

Is there anyone else besides myself who could change Caesar's mind about pardoning my brother?

BRUTUS:

(Brutus kneels)
I kiss thy hand, but not in flattery, Caesar,
Desiring thee that Publius Cimber may
Have an immediate freedom of repeal.

I kiss your hand, but not looking for favours, Caesar; asking you that Publius should be able to come back to Rome.

CAESAR:

(Caesar is surprised)
What, Brutus?

What are you thinking of, Brutus?

CASSIUS:

(Cassius kneels)
Pardon, Caesar; Caesar, pardon!
As low as to thy foot doth Cassius fall
To beg enfranchisement for Publius Cimber.

Have mercy, Caesar; Caesar, have mercy! I fall at your feet to ask you to grant freedom for Publius Cimber.

CAESAR:

I could be well moved, if I were as you;
If I could pray to move, prayers would move me;
....
I was constant Cimber should be banished,
And constant do remain to keep him so.

I could change my mind, if I were like other people; if I could beg other people to change their minds, then perhaps other people could persuade me to change mine; I thought that Cimber should be sent away, and I haven't changed my mind.

CINNA:

O Caesar-------

CAESAR:

(angrily)
Hence! Wilt thou lift up Olympus?

Get away! Would you try to lift up the great Mount Olympus?

DECIUS:

Great Caesar------

CAESAR:

Doth not Brutus bootless kneel?

Brutus is kneeling in front of me, is it doing any good?

CASCA:

Speak hands for me!

Let my hands (dagger) speak.

CAESAR:

Et tu, Brute? Then fall Caesar.

AT 2: Level 2-5

DECISIONS FOR MARK ANTONY

Mark Antony was Caesar's friend. Some people thought he was not serious. Nowadays, we might say he was:

Jack the Lad   *Hooray Henry*   *Playboy*

Mark Antony loved Caesar. Could he be cunning and clever and get revenge[1] for Caesar's death?

If you were Mark Antony, what would you do?

Below is a list of things that Mark Antony could do. Discuss them with a partner,
then write them in order, beginning with the cleverest thing(s) he could do and ending with the
things that you think would not help him to get revenge.

If I were Mark Antony I would:

Rush in and try to kill all the conspirators.

Wait and see what was going to happen.

Try to get lots of other people to fight with me against the conspirators.

Pretend to be friendly with the conspirators.

Get word to Octavius Caesar, my friend, to come to Rome immediately.

Tell Octavius Caesar to wait outside Rome until it was safe to come in.

Tell lies to get my own way. The conspirators lied too!

Try to speak at Caesar's funeral. There would be many people there.

Can you think of other things that Mark Antony might do?

[1]revenge means getting your own back. If someone hits you, you hit them. If someone plays a mean trick on you, you play a mean trick on them, to get revenge.

AT 1: Level 2-4
AT 2: Level 2-4

WHAT DID MARK ANTONY DO?

> Look at page 42 in the *Graphic Julius Caesar* and write these sentences in your notebook, filling in the spaces.

1. Mark Antony _____ _____ with the conspirators.

2. He asked to speak at Caesar's _____.

3. Brutus said, "_____ _____ , Mark Antony."

4. Cassius thought that Brutus had made a _____ decision.

Mark Antony's real feelings

> From the following sentences, choose the ones that you think best show
> Mark Antony's real feelings and write them in the speech bubble. The Key Speech, below,
> will help you. Cut out the picture and paste it in your book.

Caesar, forgive me for talking to the men who murdered you.

Brutus and Cassius are very nice people, really.

I will get revenge for Caesar's death.

Rome will be better off without Caesar.

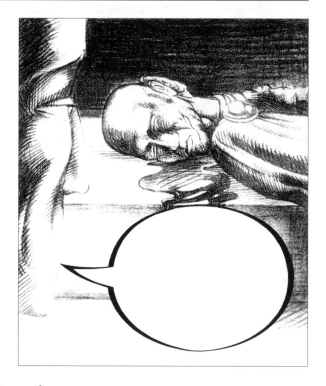

Key Speech

MARK ANTONY: O pardon me, thou bleeding piece of earth,
That I am meek and gentle with these butchers!
Thou art the ruins of the noblest man
That ever lived in the tide of times.
Woe to the hand that shed this costly blood!

Please forgive me, you bleeding lifeless thing, that I am trying to be friendly with your killers. You are the remains of the greatest man who has ever lived. I promise revenge on those whose hands stabbed you.

AT 2: Level 2-5
AT 3: Level 2

CAESAR'S FUNERAL

Key Speeches

BRUTUS: If there be any in this assembly, any dear friend of Caesar's, to him I say that Brutus' love to Caesar was no less than his. If then that friend demand why Brutus rose against Caesar, this is my answer: Not that I loved Caesar less, but that I loved Rome more. Had you rather Caesar were living, and die all slaves, than that Caesar were dead, to live all free men? As Caesar loved me, I weep for him; as he was fortunate, I rejoice at it; as he was valiant, I honour him; but, as he was ambitious, I slew him.

If there is anyone here in this gathering who was a dear friend of Caesar's, I can tell him that I loved Caesar just as much as he did. If that friend then wants to know why I helped to kill Caesar, I reply: I loved Caesar, but I loved Rome more. Would you rather have Caesar alive, and all be slaves; or have Caesar dead, and all be free men? I know that Caesar loved me, and I feel sad about his death; when he had good luck, I was happy for him; when he was brave, I admired him, but because he wanted more and more power, I killed him.

ANTONY: Friends, Romans, countrymen, lend me your ears;
I come to bury Caesar, not to praise him.
The evil that men do lives after them,
The good is oft interred with their bones;
So let it be with Caesar. The noble Brutus
Hath told you Caesar was ambitious.
If it were so, it was a grievous fault,
And grievously hath Caesar answered it.
Here, under leave of Brutus and the rest
(For Brutus is an honourable man,
So are they all, all honourable men),
Come I to speak in Caesar's funeral.

Friends, Romans, citizens, listen to me for a moment. I am here to see that Caesar is peacefully buried; I am not here to tell you he was wonderful. People remember the bad things that leaders do, while the good things they do are forgotten after they are put in the ground. It will be the same with Caesar. The good Brutus has told you that Caesar was greedy for power. If that was true, it was very serious indeed, but Caesar has had a terrible punishment for it. Brutus and the rest (Brutus is a good man, as they all are) have given me permission to come and speak in Caesar's funeral.

Good friends, sweet friends, let me not stir you up
To such a sudden flood of mutiny.

Good, dear friends, I don't want to make you angry and start a war.

For I have neither writ, nor words, nor worth,
Action, nor utterance, nor the power of speech
To stir men's blood; I only speak right on.
I tell you that which you yourselves do know,
Show you sweet Caesar's wounds, poor, poor dumb mouths,
And bid them speak for me. But were I Brutus,
And Brutus Antony, there were an Antony
Would ruffle up your spirits, and put a tongue
In every wound of Caesar that should move
The stones of Rome to rise and mutiny.

I am not good at speaking in public, sharing my feelings and making you feel angry. I only talk to you in an ordinary way. I'm really telling you what you already know, and letting you see Caesar's wounds that are like poor mouths not able to speak, yet they can say more than I can. But if I were Brutus, and Brutus were me, Antony, then I would be able to make you feel so furious that even the stones of our streets and buildings would get up and fight.

CROWD: We'll mutiny!
We'll burn the house of Brutus.
Away then! Come, seek the conspirators.

AT 2: Level 2-5

MAKING A NEWSPAPER

Of course, there would not have been newspapers in Roman times. If there had been newspapers, they might have looked something like the pages you have been given. The four pages are meant to look like a modern tabloid newspaper. A tabloid newspaper is a smaller, folded newspaper, such as the *Evening Standard*, the *Daily Mail*, and the *Daily Express*.

Some parts of the newspaper have been done for you. Your task is to
complete the newspaper articles. If you enjoy being a newspaper reporter, you might like to make
your own newspaper.

Your newspaper should have four pages.

Page 1: **Headlines about Caesar's murder and a picture of Caesar.**

Page 2: **Brutus's funeral speech. How he spoke. What the people said.**

Page 3: **Mark Antony's funeral speech. What the people said and did.**

Page 4: **Eyewitness account. An eyewitness is someone who was there at the time and saw everything with his own eyes. The eyewitness should describe the funeral speeches - first, Brutus and then Mark Antony. The eyewitness will say how she felt at the time.**

AT 2: Level 2-3
AT 3: Level 2-4

THE ROMAN TIMES

Volume 99 Issue 11   16th March

CAESAR SLAIN!

Rome Riots!

Caesar lies slain on the steps of the Capitol.

It's Civil War!

CROWDS CHEER BRUTUS, BUT...

Brutus today told the people of Rome why he and others murdered Caesar. The crowd cheered him. It was right to have got rid of Caesar! They cheered Brutus again.

These were the reasons that Brutus gave for killing Caesar:

Brutus loved _____, but loved _____ more.

If Caesar were _____, Romans would be _____,.

Now that Caesar was _____ Romans were _____

Brutus hated Caesar for being too _____.

He killed Caesar because of his _____.

He said he was ready to kill _____, if the people wished it.

The people shouted, _____, _____! _____, _____!'

Caesar   Rome   alive   slaves   dead
free men   ambitious   ambition   himself
'Live, Brutus! Live, Live!'

ANTONY WINS THEM OVER!

At first the people did not want to listen to Mark Antony. As he spoke, he made them very angry that Caesar had been murdered. They went rioting into the streets of Rome shouting, 'Death to the conspirators!'

Here are Mark Antony's reasons:

1. ....

2. ....

3. ....

Each time he gave a reason, he said, 'Brutus says he was ambitious, and Brutus is an honourable man!'

Next Mark Antony showed the crowd Caesar's _____ . He pointed out the _____ wounds. _____ gave the worst blow. It broke Caesar's heart because he had _____ Brutus.

Mark Antony read out Caesar's _____ . He had left _____ and _____ to the people of Rome.

      body   stab   Brutus
    loved   will   money   parks

WHAT THE PEOPLE SAY!

**Top Roman Times reporter, _____
was at Caesar's funeral and sent this eyewitness account.**

Brutus spoke to the crowds very _____. You could tell that he was a _____ man. He said that Caesar was too _____. Then he said he would _____ himself if the crowd asked him to.

'_____, _____!' they shouted.

Brutus had been right to kill Caesar. We didn't even want to listen to _____ _____.

quietly   good   ambitious   kill

'Live, Brutus!'   Mark Antony

Now finish the eyewitness account.

What did Mark Antony show the people?

What did he read to them?

How did the people feel when Mark Antony had finished speaking?
What did they want to do?

Why did Mark Antony feel pleased with what he had done?

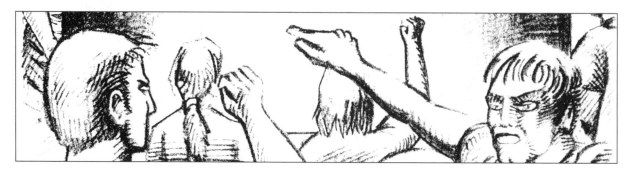

THE TRIUMVIRATE

Answer the following in your notebook. Remember to put the date and the title
at the top of your work.

What is a triumvirate?

_____

Who were the three members of the triumvirate?

1.   _____

2.   _____

3.   _____

Look at the Key Speeches.

BRUTUS:	These many then shall die; their names are pricked.	*These are the people who are to be killed; we've marked their names.*
OCTAVIUS:	Your brother too must die; consent you, Lepidus?	*Your brother must be killed, too; do you agree, Lepidus?*
LEPIDUS:	I do consent…	*I agree…*
OCTAVIUS:	Prick him down, Antony.	*Mark his name, Antony.*
LEPIDUS:	Upon condition Publius shall not live, Who is your sister's son, Mark Antony.	*On condition that we kill Publius, your nephew, your sister's son, Mark Antony.*
ANTONY:	He shall not live; look, with a spot I damn him.	*He shall be killed; look, with a mark I condemn him to death.*

Three people gather round a table with maps and lists. Read the Key Speeches together.
Read them in modern English then in Shakespeare's English. Write in your notebooks the words that
describe how they were making decisions.

The triumvirate were making decisions:

1. _____   Choose from: slowly and carefully

                                                          hastily and quickly

2. _____   after a lot of thought

                                                          with very little thought

AT 2: Level 2-4
AT 3: Level 2

BRUTUS AND CASSIUS HAD AN ARGUMENT

Choose the words that best complete the sentences below. Write the
complete sentences in your notebook. Remember to write the date and the title at the
top of your work.

1. Brutus and Cassius and their armies met and started to (*fight argue pray*).

2. Brutus said that Cassius had taken (*horses tents bribes*).

3. Cassius said that he was a more experienced (*soldier thief horseman*) than Brutus.

4. Brutus said that he was not afraid of Cassius's (*horse servant anger*).

5. Cassius was afraid he would lose his (*sword temper army*) and hurt Brutus.

6. Brutus said that Cassius had refused to send (*food money soldiers*) for Brutus's army.

7. Cassius said that the messenger was a (*fool traitor farmer*).

8. Cassius felt very (*angry hurt pleased*) at all the things Brutus said to him.

9. Cassius offered Brutus a (*cup money dagger*) to strike at his heart.

10. Brutus told Cassius to (*sharpen put away hide*) the dagger.

With a partner, read the Key Speeches below.
Remember that Brutus and Cassius are very angry.

Key Speeches

BRUTUS: Let me tell you, Cassius, you yourself
Are much condemned to have an itching palm,
To sell and mart your offices for gold
To undeserves.

*I can say, Cassius, that a lot of people think
that you are a person who takes bribes,
selling favours for money to people who
don't deserve them.*

CASSIUS: I an itching palm?
You know that you are Brutus that speaks this,
Or, by the gods, this speech were else your last.

*I, take bribes?
Only you, Brutus, can get away with
speaking to me like this; I would kill
anyone else.*

AT 2: Level 2-5
AT 3: Level 2

WHERE SHOULD THE BATTLE BE FOUGHT?

Choose the words that best complete the sentences below. Write the
sentences in your notebook. Remember to write the date and the title at the
top of your work.

Key Speeches

BRUTUS: O Cassius, I am sick of many griefs.   *O Cassius, I have so many things on my*
               …Portia is dead.   *mind, I feel ill.*

CASSIUS: Ha? Portia?

BRUTUS: She is dead.

CASSIUS: How scaped I killing when I crossed you so?   *I'm surprised you didn't kill me, getting*
               O insupportable and touching loss!   *angry with you at a time like this. An*
               Upon what sickness?   *unbearable loss. What caused her death?*

Was this a good time for Brutus to make an important decision?
Choose one of the following and give a good reason:

Yes, it was a good time for Brutus to make and important decision, because

_____

or

No, it was not a good time for Brutus to make an important decision, because

_____

What did Cassius think they should do?

_____

_____

What did Brutus think they should do?

_____

_____

Who got his own way?   _____

Caesar's ghost

What is a **ghost**? Caesar was dead. Brutus saw something that looked and spoke like Caesar – Caesar come
back from the dead. A ghost. People in Shakespeare's day believed in ghosts. Many people do nowadays.

Look at the Key Speeches on p.59. Caesar's words had two meanings. Write them in your notebook.

CAESAR: Thou shalt see me at Philippi.

1.   Caesar's ghost would appear again to Brutus on the battlefield.
2.   Brutus would die. Therefore, they would both be ghosts.

Do you think the ghost wanted to help Brutus or frighten him? Choose which, and explain why.

AT 2: Level 2-5
AT 3: Level 2-3

DIARY OF A SOLDIER- PART 1

A diary is a daily record of what happens in a person's life. The diary below shows what an ordinary soldier in Brutus's army might have written. First, fill in the spaces with the words that are given to help you. Next try to write a page on your own. Can you imagine how the ordinary soldier felt? You could keep your own diary for a few days. If you have any problems, writing them down sometimes helps to sort them out.

I joined Brutus's _____ . Brutus was a _____ man, and I wanted to

help him. I thought he was _____ to get rid of Caesar. Caesar was

getting too _____. First, we marched to _____. There

were a lot of problems about _____ and where our _____ was

coming from. There was never _____ food. Sometimes people

fought over _____. There weren't enough tents. Some people

wrapped themselves in their cloaks and slept on the _____ .

army   good   right   powerful

Sardis   money   food

enough   food   ground

Can you write another page of the diary?

Brutus and Cassius had an argument. How would the soldiers feel?

What did Brutus say that Cassius had done?

How would the soldiers feel when they were told to march to Philippi?

Write about these things in your diary.

AT 2: Level 2-4
AT 3: Level 2

THE PLAINS OF PHILIPPI

Page 60 in the *Graphic Julius Caesar* will help you to do the work below.
Don't forget to write the date when you begin a new piece of work, and underline the titles. This work in your notebook will help you to revise for tests. Have you tried to memorise any of the Key Speeches?

The **plains** means a flat, grassy place – a good place for a battle.

The four leaders met on the battlefield at Philippi.

On one side were Brutus and _____.

On the other side were Mark Antony and _____.

They spoke _____ to each other.

These speeches will be loud and angry.
They want all their soldiers to hear what they are saying.

Key Speeches

BRUTUS: Words before blows; is it so, countrymen?

OCTAVIUS: Not that we love words better, as you do.

BRUTUS: Good words are better than bad strokes,
               Octavius.

ANTONY: In your bad strokes, Brutus, you give good
               words;
               Witness the hole you made in Caesar's heart,
               Crying, 'Long live! Hail, Caesar!'

Brutus's decisions

Look at page 60. Can you find the three important decisions made by Brutus?
Write them in your notebook and after each one write: *A good decision for the conspirators* or *A bad decision for the conspirators* or *Not known yet*. Explain the reason for your answer.

1. _____
   _____

2. _____
   _____

3. _____
   _____

AT 2: Level 2-5
AT 3: Level 2-4

BRUTUS AND CASSIUS SAID GOODBYE

Read the Key Speeches on page 63 with a partner. They are not difficult to understand.
Read them together, remembering that this is a quiet moment in the play. Write the sentences below
in your notebook.

Brutus and Cassius spoke _____ the battle. They had a feeling that they might not _____.

Would it be better to be taken _____, or to _____ themselves?

They said _____ to each other.

THE BATTLE

Pages 64 to 70 describe the battle. Here is an outline of what happened.
Copy it into your notebook.

1.   Romans were fighting _____ . It was very hard to know who were _____ and who

       were _____ .

2.   Cassius thought that his friend _____ was taken prisoner. He thought they were _____

       the battle.

3.   Cassius covered his face and Pindarus killed him with the _____ .

4.   Titinius and Messala found Cassius's body. _____ had not been taken prisoner after all!

       Cassius had killed himself because of a _____.

5.   Titinius was so _____ that he killed himself as well.

6.   Cassius was _____ ; _____ had to fight on alone.

7.   Brutus realised that the _____ was lost. He did not want to be taken _____ .

8.   Strato held the _____ and Brutus ran upon it and died.

9.   Going to Philippi had been another _____ decision.

10.   _____ _____ said about Brutus: 'THIS WAS THE NOBLEST ROMAN OF THEM ALL.'

AT 3: Level 2

DIARY OF A SOLDIER – PART 2

Here is another page of your soldier's diary. Complete it as you did the first one,
then write a further page in your own words.
How would the soldier feel when the battle was over? Remember he had fought for Brutus,
and thought Brutus was a good man.

We had a long march to _____. Everyone felt very worried about

Brutus's and Cassius's bad _____ .

When we got to Philippi, we were very _____ .

The two great armies met on the _____ . Romans were against

_____ . It seemed _____ .

Our leader, Brutus, and Cassius met Mark Antony and Octavius. They spoke

_____ to each other. The _____ began.

Philippi	*quarrel*	*tired*	*battlefield*
Romans	*wrong*	*angrily*	*battle*

Finish the soldier's diary of the battle.

There would be a lot of noise.

He would see very bad wounds.

He would hear about Cassius and Brutus killing themselves.

How would he feel during the battle?

How would he feel when the battle was over?

AT 3: Level 2-4

The 'Who am I?' Game

You need 5 activity sheets for this game, including this one. Prepare for the 'Who Am I' game as follows:

1.   Paste each set of character clues onto a separate card.

2.   Add the appropriate portrait from the Picture Gallery.

3.   Number the cards, the order is not important. (eg. 1. Brutus   2. Caesar   3. Cassius   etc.)

4.   Make up individual score cards as follows:

NAME:		
CARD No.	POINTS SCORED	TOTAL
	GRAND TOTAL	

Rules of the Game

1.   Working in pairs, one student holds the card with the blank side facing the partner. The partner asks questions that can be answered 'Yes' or 'No'.

   For example: 'Are you a man?'
                    'Are you a conspirator?'

2.   Each question counts as one point.

3.   Each direct question about the name of a character counts 5 points if the answer is 'No'.
   For example: 'Are you Calphurnia?' counts 5 points if the answer is no. This is to stop pupils simply guessing, hoping to get lucky!

4.   Clues may be offered, one at a time, in return for a small 'price' of two points.
   At the request, 'Please give me a clue', one of the clues on the card is read out, and two points are added to the score.

5.   Mark the points on your score card as you go along. Add up the points on each line for the 'Total' column as you identify each character.

Take turns holding the cards and asking the questions. Remember, the aim is to guess the name of the character while getting the **lowest** number of points.

CHARACTER CLUES • 1

Julius Caesar

Paste portrait here

> I was winning battles. I beat Pompey.
> I was popular with the people.
> Some people thought I was getting too powerful.
> The people offered me a crown. I refused it.
> My wife, Calphurnia, had terrible dreams.
> Some foolish soothsayer tried to tell me that I should be careful on the ides of March.
> Brutus was my friend, I trusted him.
> I thought Cassius was too thin. I didn't trust him.
> When Brutus stabbed me, that was the end.

Brutus

Paste portrait here

> Caesar was my friend. He trusted me.
> People wrote to me. They said I had to do something about Caesar.
> I thought Caesar was getting too powerful.
> I loved my wife, Portia.
> I had a lot of arguments with Cassius.
> I spoke at Caesar's funeral.
> I thought we should fight at Philippi.
> I saw Caesar's ghost.
> I had to fight on alone after Cassius killed himself.
> I was a conspirator.

Cassius

Paste portrait here

> I hated Caesar. He was getting too powerful.
> Caesar wasn't so great. I had seen that he could be weak.
> I sent Brutus fake letters. It was easy to fool him.
> I wanted to kill Mark Antony when he killed Caesar.
> I didn't want Mark Antony to speak at Caesar's funeral.
> I thought it was stupid to go to Philippi.
> I was the first conspirator.

Mark Antony

Paste portrait here

> Some people thought I was too fond of parties.
> Caesar told me he didn't trust Cassius.
> After the conspirators killed Caesar, I pretended to be nice to them.
> I made the people really angry with Brutus and Cassius.
> I found Caesar's will and read it to the people.
> I started a riot in Rome!
> Octavius, Lepidus and I made a triumvirate.
> Octavius and I fought Brutus and Cassius at Philippi.

CHARACTER CLUES • 2

Calphurnia

Paste portrait
here

> I was Caesar's wife.
> I had terrible dreams the night before Caesar was murdered.
> Decius Brutus said that my dream had a good meaning.
> I didn't want Caesar to go to the Capitol on the ides of March.

Portia

Paste portrait
here

> I was Brutus's wife.
> I didn't like the men who came to see Brutus.
> Brutus and I talked together in our garden.
> Brutus said he would tell me everything later.
> Brutus and I loved each other very much.
> After Caesar was killed, I was very worried about Brutus.
> In the end, I killed myself.

Casca

Paste portrait
here

> I met Brutus and Cassius. They were having a serious talk.
> I told Brutus and Cassius how Mark Antony offered Caesar a crown.
> I saw Caesar refuse the crown.
> It seemed to me Caesar really wanted the crown.
> Caesar, a king? What a load of rubbish!
> I gave the signal to kill Caesar.
> I shouted, 'Speak, hands, for me!'

Decius Brutus

Paste portrait
here

> I persuaded Caesar to go to the Capitol on the ides of March.
> Calphurnia had a bad dream about Caesar.
> I told Calphurnia that her dream had a good meaning.
> I said that if Caesar didn't go out, people would laugh at him.
> I was a conspirator.

Cinna

Paste portrait
here

> I was one of the first conspirators.
> I joined Casca and Cassius.
> I put three fake letters where Brutus would find them.

CHARACTER CLUES • 3

Flavius or Marullus Paste portrait here	> I was a tribune. > The people were celebrating Caesar's victory over Pompey. I was very angry. > I told the tradesmen to go home. > I pulled the decorations off Caesar's statues. > I thought Caesar was getting too powerful.

The Soothsayer Paste portrait here	> Sometimes, I know what is going to happen in the future. > I knew the ides of March would be a bad day for Caesar. > I tried to warn Caesar. He said I was a dreamer. > I saw Caesar on the ides of March. He laughed at me.

Artemidorus Paste portrait here	> I found out about the plot to kill Caesar. > I made a list of all the conspirators. I tried to give it to Caesar. > There were too many people around Caesar. > Caesar wouldn't read my list.

Octavius Paste portrait here	> I was Caesar's nephew. > After Caesar was killed, Mark Antony told me to wait outside Rome. > Mark Antony told me when it was safe to enter Rome. > Mark Antony, Lepidus and I made a triumvirate. > Our triumvirate put a lot of people on the list to be killed. > Mark Antony and I beat Cassius and Brutus at Philippi.

PORTRAIT GALLERY

Cut around dotted lines and paste portraits on to the character clue cards.

Julius Caesar

Calphurnia

Brutus

Portia

Cassius

Mark Anthony

Casca

Cinna

Decius Brutus

Octavius

Flavius

Marullus

Soothsayer

Artemidorus

YOU ARE THE EDITOR

You need 2 activity pages for this task. They show some newspaper headlines that might have been written as the play took place. Cut them out and paste them into your notebook in the right order.

MOBS LOOT ROME

BRUTUS TO SPEAK AT CAESAR'S FUNERAL

STRANGE NIGHT IN ROME
WEIRD SIGHTS ARE SEEN

BATTLE RAGES AT PHILIPPI

DEFEAT FOR POMPEY!
VICTORY FOR CAESAR!

CAESAR MURDERED!

CASSIUS DEAD! BRUTUS DEAD!
CONSPIRATORS DEFEATED!

BRUTUS WEEPS FOR PORTIA!

"BEWARE THE IDES OF MARCH"
Soothsayer tells Caesar

LONG MARCH FROM SARDIS TO PHILIPPI

TRIUMVIRATE RULES ROME

MARK ANTONY TELLS ALL: CROWD GOES MAD

LONG LIVE MARK ANTONY LONG LIVE OCTAVIUS PEACE RETURNS TO ROME

Choose a headline and make a page of a newspaper, following the model on pages 27-30.
Write the news story to go with it. Add a picture if you wish.

THE KARATE KID

Work in pairs. One student is to be the teacher or *sensei*, the other is the pupil, the *Karate Kid*.

Choose one of the longer, more difficult Key Speeches. First read the speech in modern English, then in Shakespeare's language. The *sensei* tries to make sure that the pupil, the *Karate Kid*, has a good understanding of the speech.

Next, the *Karate Kid* will practise reading the speech in Shakespeare's English, using actions and speaking with expression. The *sensei* will make helpful suggestions and perhaps demonstrate how the speech can be read.

Write the speech on a piece of card (or cut it out and paste it on if you wish). Mark the places where you want to pause and perhaps underline the most important words.

The *Karate Kid(s)* will then perform their speeches for their classmates. The best *Karate Kids* will have the best *senseis*.

Example:

CAESAR:	<u>Cowards</u> die many times before their deaths; The <u>valiant</u> never taste death but once. Of all the wonders that I yet have heard, It seems to me most strange that men should fear, <u>Seeing that death, a necessary end,</u> <u>Will come when it will come.</u>	 *Pause* *Speaking slowly*

Note: You may use the Key Speeches in the *Graphic Julius Caesar*, or you can choose a longer speech from the play.

Who's Who?

Cut out the pictures of the characters below. They are: *Cassius, Caesar, Calphurnia, Portia, Brutus, Casca, Soothsayer, Mark Antony*. Paste them into your notebook with a few lines between each one.

Here are some things that the people might say about themselves. Can you match the sentences with the right faces? Write them underneath. Some of the characters will have quite a lot of sentences; others might have only one.

I had terrible dreams that night before Caesar went to the Capitol.

When I spoke at Caesar's funeral, I made the people really angry.

I appeared to Brutus after I was dead!

It was very difficult for me to decide to join the plan to kill Caesar. He was my friend.

I hated Caesar. He had become very powerful, but I knew he was weak.

I saw Mark Antony offer Caesar the crown, to be King of Rome. What a load of rubbish.

I loved Brutus very much. I killed myself because of all the trouble he got into.

I spoke to the people at Caesar's funeral. I explained very carefully why we had to kill him.

I told Caesar to expect trouble on the fifteenth of March.

Can you make up some more sentences like these and write them under the pictures? Talk about your ideas with a partner.

Cassius

Julius Caesar

Calphurnia

Portia

Brutus

Casca

Soothsayer

Mark Anthony

JULIUS CAESAR

RECORD OF MY WORK

Name: _____

Date started: _____

Form: _____

Date completed: _____

TITLE AND NUMBER OF ACTIVITY	How well did you do this activity?			Was it easy or difficult?			TEACHER'S OR PUPIL'S COMMENTS
	Very Well	Quite Well	I could have tried harder	Too difficult	Too easy	Just right	

WHAT THINGS HAVE I IMPROVED?

Writing in sentences	Using full stops and capital letters	Spelling	Understanding Shakespeare's English	Acting and speaking Shakespeare's English	What did I enjoy about *Julius Caesar*?	What went well with my work?	How can I do better?